This book is dedicated to whom we met online via personal ads we placed.

Who knew such great men were waiting for us?

Karin's husband, John

Beth's husband, Warren

FINDING YOUR MATE ONLINE:

NO FEAR,
NO EMBARRASSMENT,
JUST LOVE!

by
Karin Sterling Anderson
&
Beth Roberts

Published by Just Show Me What to Do, LLC
www.justshowmewhat2do.com

Printed and bound by Booksurge, LLC
in the United States of America

For more information, visit us at:

www.justshowmewhat2do.com

CONTENTS

JUST <u>SHOW</u> ME WHAT TO DO: VISUAL GUIDES FOR WOMEN

**Have you ever wished:
"If only a woman had designed this!"**

Imagine living in a world where the cure for
cellulite was eating chocolate . . .

. . . men loved cleaning as much as sex . . .

. . . and shopping for shoes
was medically prescribed!

Imagine easy and fun guidebooks on *every* subject, especially
intimidating ones like online dating, investing, childcare and buying
a home.

Finally, women have designed a series of guidebooks especially for
women. We make your life easier by . . .

> • Using pictures along with text to teach. It's the difference
> between *Vogue* and your Calculus college textbook. Not only are
> women the more visual sex, but isn't a picture worth a thousand
> words?

> • Allowing you to pick the *starting point* in any book.
> You know best whether you are a Beginner, Intermediate or
> Advanced in any subject. Why waste time reading information
> you already know?

INTRODUCTION

Karin

Whenever I need a how-to book, I head for the children's section. Open any children's instructional book and you'll see fun pictures that make learning entertaining! Something happens to books when they grow up. The pictures, simplicity and joy disappear, replaced by tiny print and too much information! Serious and deadly boring. Who deserves entertaining books more than adults toiling in an office all day?

Beth

I'm one of those adults toiling all day in an office in front of my computer. A lawyer by trade, text documents are my life. When I go home at night, the last thing I want to do is read a boring how-to book! I do, however, want to keep up with the world and learn new things in a fun way. I don't have a lot of extra time, and the free time I DO have, I don't want to feel like work! I'm the tail end of the baby-boomer generation, one of many working professionals. If I feel like this, there must be many others out there who do, too.

We developed the book series **Just <u>Show</u> Me What To Do: Visual Guides For Women** for everyone to use. Although these techniques can be successfully used by both sexes, we felt more comfortable writing for women because we know what women like. We may think we know what pleases men, but they're still a big mystery!

This particular guidebook, *Finding Your Mate Online*, developed from personal experience as we both met our husbands online.

Beth, you make it sound so easy. Remember how we both desperately needed *Finding Your Mate Online: No Fear, No Embarrassment, Just Love*! when we wanted to post a personal ad online? We spent years looking at and commenting on other people's ads, but it took many months—

—and glasses of wine . . .

—to gather the nerve to put our pictures and desires into cyberspace.

I loved the voyeur part; it was great fun reading the ads posted by others. I had a harder time getting used to the idea of actually putting my money where my mouth was—the thought of responding to someone's ad, or placing my own, made my stomach queasy. It took me six months to muster the courage to finally place my personal ad online. However, once online, I made up for lost time. The fifth man I met is now my husband.

It took me a bit longer, but the end justifies the means. My husband is identical to the wish list I created, and I've never been happier.

What follows is our visual guide to online dating. With these fun pictures and easy explanations, we hope to make this educational tool feel fresh and fun. This book will help you get past any prior intimidation. More importantly, we hope to eliminate any fears or shame about online dating. Remember—*you can't win if you don't play!*

— Authors Karin Sterling Anderson and Beth Roberts

HOW BEST TO USE OUR BOOKS

(This is a different kind of book, but with differences you'll grow to love!)

The first difference you will love about our series of guidebooks—
Just <u>Show</u> Me What To Do: Visual Guides For Women—is our
use of VISUALS and text to teach—think adult comic books. For
example, know what the strip at the top of your computer screen
with all the symbols for shortcuts on it is called? The one you refer
to as *"the doohickey at the top of your screen?"*

The proper name is actually **toolbar,** but since you call it *"the
doohickey at the top of your screen,"* confusion and frustration will
result when trying to follow instructions.

But when we **just <u>show</u> you** a picture of a toolbar . . .

. . . you understand immediately! There's no room for error and
frustration.

The second difference you will love is how we've divided the
guidebooks into three sections: BEGINNING, INTERMEDIATE and
ADVANCED. Why waste precious time reading what you already
know to get to what you really need to know?

These innovative and fun guidebooks will do you no good, however,
unless you use them! As our fathers used to say, **"The successful
people are willing to do what the unsuccessful are unwilling
to do."**

You are going to successfully find your mate online without fear or
embarrassment because you are willing to follow the guidelines in
this book!

FUN AND FRIENDLY GUIDES

You'll find helpful icons throughout our book series that will come to feel like familiar friends as they guide you along.

RULE OF THUMB

This helpful thumbs-up identifies basic rules to follow and take to heart.

HELPFUL HINT

Our lightbulb will give you helpful pointers and advice!

WWW

Whenever you see the WWW for the World Wide Web, we'll guide you to our website for additional help and also forms you can download.

AUTHOR'S ADVICE

True stories from the trenches! Learn from our mistakes and successes.

TAKE A BREATH!

Take some downtime to reflect and clear your mind whenever we remind you to take a breath!

SECTION ONE

BEGINNER

Getting Online & Posting Your Ad

WHEN SHOULD YOU START WITH THE BEGINNER SECTION?

WHEN THE COMPUTER'S SCARY . . .

If you're intimidated by the computer,
we can get you online!

Turn to page 5

"GETTING ONLINE"

WHEN PLACING
AN AD'S SCARY . . .

If you're computer savvy, but need help finding dating sites or creating an ad, start with the BEGINNER SECTION

—but skip the GETTING ONLINE section—

and turn to page 15.

GETTING ONLINE

WHAT YOU'LL NEED

To find your mate online, you'll need:

1.   A computer

2.   An Internet Service Provider
(a.k.a. I.S.P.) like AOL, Earthlink, MSN, etc.

RULE OF THUMB

ALWAYS USE YOUR
HOME COMPUTER

DON'T use your work computer for online dating. Most companies have strict policies against using company property for personal use.

Employers have the right to check their network records to see where and when you went online.

NO HOME COMPUTER?

Don't have a home computer?

Can't afford a home computer?

MANY *NON-WORK* OPTIONS ARE AVAILABLE:

Library

Cyber-café

Copy Center

WOMAN ON THE GO?

What if you're traveling and don't have access
to your home computer?

STILL MANY NON-WORK OPTIONS ARE AVAILABLE:

Hotel

Cyber-café

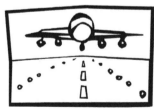

Airport

ALONG WITH A COMPUTER, YOU'LL NEED AN I.S.P.

Internet

Service

Provider

THINK OF AN I.S.P. AS:

How you travel online!

Just as there are many vehicles . . .

Car

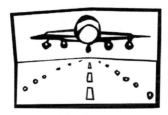

Airplane

Bicycle

There are many I.S.P.s out there.

WHICH I.S.P.?

Choose one with unlimited access time. Most have toll-free numbers and can sign you up over the phone. Some of the most popular:

AOL, EARTHLINK and MSN

HELPFUL HINT

Choose the same I.S.P. that a knowledgeable friend or family member uses. You'll have them to ask for help and advice, in addition to the I.S.P.'s technical support.

CONGRATULATIONS!
YOU CAN GET ONLINE!
NOW . . . *WHERE TO GO?*

FIRST STEP: ORGANIZE

We know you want to get started ASAP, but you'll thank us
later for being organized!

First, you're going to create folders on your computer
for storing all the information you'll need and receive in
connection with your online personal ad (your LISTS and
PICTURES, for starters).

This is just like filing papers and pictures in manila folders in
a metal filing cabinet.

W W W

Free website for book purchasers!

Need help creating folders?

We've listed helpful instructions on CREATING FOLDERS and other technical requirements on our website:

www.justshowmewhat2do.com/books

Just Show Me What To Do has its own website that provides you with all sorts of free tips and information to supplement this book.

HOW DO I GET THERE?

Type:

www.justshowmewhat2do.com

into the "location bar"

at the top of your computer.

Then either click on GO by the location bar or ENTER (or RETURN) on the keyboard.

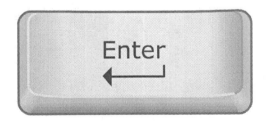

WHAT WILL SHOW UP
ON YOUR COMPUTER:

Then enter and click on the BOOKS button:

DON'T SWEAT THE COMPUTER STUFF

Creating folders will either be a familiar process or not.

If doing anything on the computer other than sending email seems foreign, ask a computer-savvy friend or a teenager for help.

There's no shame in not knowing everything about a computer! Whatever you do, don't be intimidated and don't stop!

THE METAL FILING CABINET

Now that you have mastered the skill of creating folders on your computer (*or someone's mastered it for you*), create one and call it "THE SEARCH."

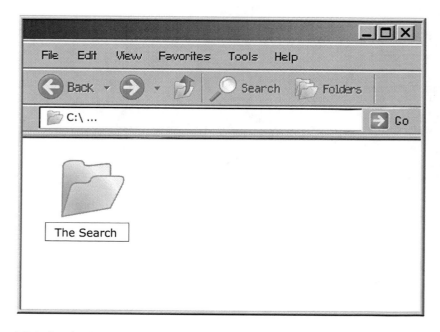

Think of THE SEARCH as the metal filing cabinet where you're going to store all your information about your search for finding your mate online!

Note: THE SEARCH may be one of many folders on your hard drive.

ORGANIZING "THE SEARCH"

Now we need to create folders within THE SEARCH to store various information we'll have you gather throughout this book.

Click on the folder icon you named THE SEARCH.

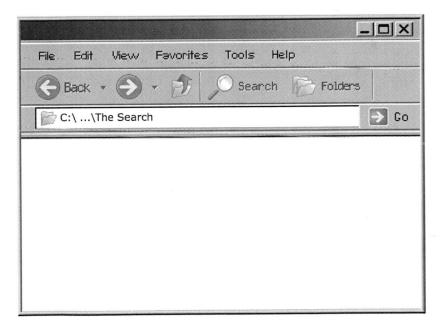

Now you're inside it!

INSIDE "THE SEARCH"

Once inside, create the following folders:

LISTS and PICTURES

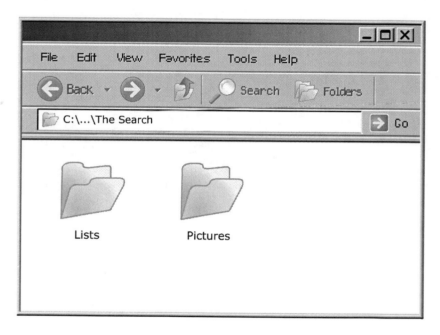

As we progress through this section, we'll show you how
to fill each of these folders with what you need to help you
prepare an awesome online dating ad.

LISTS, LISTS, LISTS!

In real estate, the three most important elements are

location, location, location

In online dating, the three most important elements are

lists, lists, lists

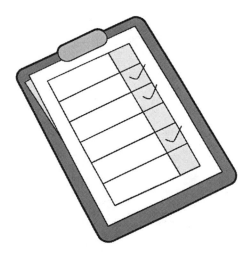

THE KEYS TO SUCCESS: CREATING *YOUR* LISTS!

We've created three lists for you to use as reference tools in preparing your ad.

We know that once you've got your lists in hand, you'll be able to more clearly see who you are, what you're looking for in a man (as opposed to the clichés we all fall back on) and how to turn that into an ad that works for you!

LISTS PROVIDE CLARITY

Most online dating sites ask you to fill out a questionnaire or write out characteristics of the man you're looking for.

With our lists in hand, you become more focused about what you're looking for in your mate and can easily fill out any online questionnaire and sift through replies to your ad to eliminate the wrong guys, and focus on finding Mr. Right.

WHY LISTS ARE KEY

You wouldn't you go to the grocery store to shop for an important dinner without a list of ingredients for the recipe you're making, would you?

So don't go to an online dating service without a list of qualities you want in your mate.

AUTHOR'S ADVICE

*Making a list was such an eye-opening experience for me!
I realized for the first time the huge difference between what I really
wanted and the type of men I was choosing. Once I made my list, it
was less than two weeks before I met my future husband.*

—Beth

Finally . . . a man who shares my passion for skiing! Our *list* of
destinations includes Lake Tahoe, California.

Free website for book purchasers!

Our first list requires you to find your favorite online dating site to review and take notes on various ads.

Don't have a favorite site?

Go to our website:

www.justshowmewhat2do.com/books

. . . for helpful information on the most popular sites, as well as other helpful information!

WE SHOW YOU THE POPULAR SITES:

You can check out where other people
are posting their ads!

Visit

www.justshowmewhat2do.com/books

We're always checking the latest sites for you!

HOW TO GET THERE

You can get to dating websites two ways:

1.   Enter the dating site address, a.k.a. URL, into the location bar, as described on page 17.

2.   Go to our website, and on the BOOKS page, click on the icon for our FREE DOWNLOAD, which will guide you to helpful information about online dating, including the most popular dating sites.

WHICH DATING SITE IS BEST?

There's no right answer. Browse several online dating sites to find the one where YOU feel most comfortable. Check both the men's and women's ads.

CHECK THE ADS & MAKE IT FUN!

Go to the different sites to check out the ads and the people who post them. Is this your kind of place? Are these your kind of people? Invite a close female and also a male friend to help you navigate the various sites you'll visit. Order a pizza and share your thoughts as you search and review men's and women's ads on the different sites!

FIND YOUR FAVORITE

Just like you have a favorite fashion magazine—you prefer *Elle* over *Vogue*—you'll find an online dating site that works best for you.

HELPFUL HINT

Be aware — all sites have a cost – whether directly to the
person placing the ad, the recipient, both or via the hidden
cost of gathering your information for marketing purposes.
Look for the sites that allow you to browse for a short period
of time at a minimal cost before you make a commitment.

LIST #1—ABOUT THE ADS

Our first list we call "ABOUT THE ADS." Once you've found your favorite website, take some time to take notes on the different ads there.

Use our ABOUT THE ADS list to identify what you like, and what you think doesn't work.

Other people's ads can give you clues as to what you would like your ad to look and sound like, and help shape your own ad by example.

PHOTOS AND TEXT: MEN AND WOMEN

Look at all kinds of ads, both men's and women's: Take a look at their photos as well as their words.

What do you think looks and sounds *good?*

What do you think looks and sounds *bad?*

You're trying to get a sense of what will work best for you, so be objective, and look for "DO NOT'S" as well as "DO'S"!

LIST #1: "ABOUT THE ADS"

(MAKE SURE YOU LOOK AT 20 MEN'S ADS AND 20 WOMEN'S ADS)

1. My impressions from ads found on _____.com ___, 200___.

2. The men's ads I was attracted to contained these characteristics or words: _____

3. Certain men's ads turned me off because: _____
_____

4. The women's ads I admired used these characteristics or words:
_____

5. Certain women's ads turned me off because: _____

6. Certain women's photos I liked a lot because: _____

7. Certain women's photos I didn't like at all because: _____

8. The headings I liked were: _____

9. Other notes for my ad: _____

ONCE YOU FINISH FILLING OUT THIS LIST,
SAVE IT IN YOUR "LISTS" FOLDER
THAT IS WITHIN "THE SEARCH" FOLDER.

REMEMBER TO STAY ORGANIZED!

It doesn't matter whether you download the list from our website or retype your own or even photocopy the list from our book, you'll want to start this journey being organized!

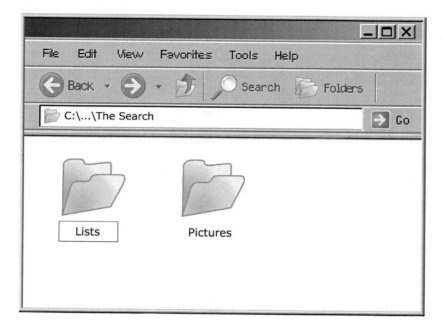

File the ABOUT THE ADS list in the LISTS folder you've created on your computer, or even file it the old-fashioned way in a paper folder!

AUTHOR'S ADVICE

I asked my best friend and her husband for help, figuring Jack would bow out after the first few minutes, but he really got into it. He offered amazing insight into how men think and advice when I was writing my ads. I've always thought my best friend was "lucky" to have found Jack, but never thought to ask for his help in finding a great guy like him!

—Karin

Our first year together—Visiting John in London when he worked as Tour Manager for Joe Strummer and The Mescaleros.

LIST #1 IS DONE!

REFLECTIVE TIME

A celebration's in order! You've found your favorite site, you can navigate through it with ease and you've completed your first list.

That's a good start. Now, take some reflective time by yourself to prepare for your next list assignments—to figure out what you want and what you have to offer.

GETTING TO KNOW YOU

You're going to need the info from your reflective time in order to complete the next section.

We're going to help you organize your thoughts so that you can go to your online dating website and create a personal ad that reflects the TRUE YOU!

HONESTY IS THE BEST POLICY!

The next two lists—ABOUT ME and ABOUT HIM—work best only if you are honest with yourself.

No one's going to read these lists but you anyway!

Everyone has room for improvement and these lists will help you pinpoint exactly where you can improve in your relationships.

LIST #2: ABOUT ME

Our second list we call "ABOUT ME." Here's where you need to refer back to your reflective time and see what you discovered about yourself.

The questions on our list are designed to help identify patterns of success and/or failure.

They also should help you come up with some buzz words to use in your ad that really define who you are.

REMEMBER—BE HONEST!

The point of this exercise is to get to the root of your dating bad habits!   You can avoid repeating them once you've posted the ad we're helping you create.

If you take the time to reflect, you'll begin to see the patterns of men you've dated—the good and the bad.

Once the patterns reveal themselves, pay attention to them!

LIST #2: "ABOUT ME"

TO DOWNLOAD THIS LIST, GO TO OUR WEBSITE:
www.justshowmewhat2do.com/books

(WHAT HAS WORKED AND WHAT HASN'T WORKED IN THE PAST)

1. In my failed relationships, the consistent problems in the *men* I pick are: _____

2. In my failed relationships, the consistent mistakes *I* make are:

_____

3. My traits that contribute to my greatness are: _____

_____

4. My traits that contribute to my weakness are: _____

_____

5. I asked 3 of my close friends for 3 adjectives to describe me:

Friend 1: _____

Friend 2: _____

Friend 3: _____

6. I will meet my mate within the next _____ months.

**ONCE YOU FINISH FILLING OUT THIS LIST,
SAVE IT IN YOUR "LISTS" FOLDER
THAT IS WITHIN "THE SEARCH" FOLDER.**

DONE WITH YOU!

Now that you've finished identifying what does or doesn't work for you, it's time to look at the men in your life.

You've chosen all the men in your life consciously and subconsciously. Since they haven't worked for you, it's time to figure out why.

Our List #3 will give you a razor focus in attracting replies to your ad from the type of men you're consciously choosing for reasons that work for you!

LIST #3   ABOUT HIM

Our third list we call "ABOUT HIM."

With Lists #1 & #2, you learned what ads you like and don't like, and now you know what does and doesn't work for you.

With List #3, you'll learn what you're looking for in a man.

No excuses, no exceptions.

THINK IT THROUGH

The List you create for "ABOUT HIM" is going to answer a lot of questions . . . all of them geared toward helping you realize what you're looking for in your mate.

Take your time, think it through, answer openly and objectively.

No sense fooling yourself . . .

Honesty truly is the best policy in finding your mate!

LIST #3:   "ABOUT HIM"

(TAKE YOUR TIME FILLING THIS OUT! IF YOU NEED MORE SPACE,
COPY AND PASTE ADDITIONAL LINES. THE MORE YOU OUTLINE
HERE, THE MORE YOU FINE-TUNE YOUR SEARCH FOR YOUR MATE!)

1.   I am looking for a partner for
   a.   Dating only. Someone to have fun with on weekends.
        I'm not ready for a serious relationship.
   b.   Marriage but no children.
   c.   Marriage and _____(#) of children.

2.   In a letter to my best friend, where I hold nothing back, I
describe him as _____
_____.

3.   On a typical weekend, we really enjoy doing _____
on a Friday night, then _____ on a Saturday,
then _____ on a Sunday.

4.   His looks remind me of _____.

5.   He's _____ years old.

6.   As far as health, he's _____.

7.   His spiritual/religious beliefs are _____.

8.   He wants _____ kids.

9.   He already has _____ kids.

10. He's been married _____ times.

11. His career is _____.

12. His attitude about money is _____.

13. His attitude toward his family is _____.

14. He treats me _____.

15. When I tell him I'd like to spend a romantic evening, we do

_____.

16. His politics are _____.

17. He treats female friends, co-workers and acquaintances like

_____.

18. I'm proud to have him as my boyfriend when _____

_____.

19. My parents like him because _____.

20. My siblings like him because _____.

21. My friends like him because _____.

22. I love him because _____

_____.

ONCE YOU FINISH FILLING OUT THIS LIST,
SAVE IT IN YOUR "LISTS" FOLDER
THAT IS WITHIN "THE SEARCH" FOLDER.

YOUR EMOTIONS ARE
IN A WHIRLWIND!

Who knew just writing about yourself and your desires could be so exhausting?

Of course it's hard . . . you're laying the groundwork for finding the best mate for you to last a lifetime.

It's an exciting time. You've just finished the blueprints for the future you've always dreamed of!

FEEDBACK IS ESSENTIAL

After you've filled out the ABOUT ME and ABOUT HIM lists, let them sit a couple of days.

Then ask someone who both knows you and will be honest with you—your best friend, your sibling, your therapist—for any thoughts or suggestions they might have for you. If their suggestions make sense, revise your lists accordingly.

NEXT STEP: CREATE A NEW SCREEN NAME!

ALREADY HAVE ONE?

WHY A *NEW* NAME?

It's a chance to reveal something about yourself to potential mates that you've learned from your lists!

scuba girl

animal lover

RULE OF THUMB

You want a new screen name, because you want to be able to abandon that screen name at any time!

Some examples:

1. You may not like some of the responses to the ad you placed and you don't want those people contacting you after you've said goodbye.

2. Once you find your mate you don't want old dates contacting you.

It's just like changing your phone number. You give the new number to people you want to hear from and you don't have to worry about people you don't want to hear from.

HELPFUL HINT

1. With some I.S.P.s, like AOL and Earthlink, you can create multiple names at no additional charge within your one account.

2. If the above option isn't available, and/or you'd rather keep your search more private, you can create FREE email accounts via **yahoo**, **hotmail**, **msn**, etc.

SAMPLE SCREEN NAMES

Babyblues@

(Everyone tells you that you have beautiful blue eyes.)

Jazz Fan @

(Your taste runs from Miles Davis to Cassandra Wilson.)

Love2Sail@

(You love spending your weekends on the water.)

PrettyCreative@

(You're an art teacher.)

SCREEN NAME DONE?
NOW, CREATE YOUR PHOTOS.

A PHOTO IS A MUST!

NOT YET PICTURED

Don't place or respond to an ad without picture(s)!

Physical attraction plays a big part in selecting a mate. Offering and getting a photo up front saves you valuable time.

No photo indicates that the person really isn't serious about online dating.

WHAT TYPE OF PHOTO?

Take a new picture. Have a friend, preferably with a digital camera, take many shots of you outside during the golden hour—the light prior to sunset when everyone looks like a movie star!

WHY NOT MY BEST PHOTO?

Here's one instance where you *shouldn't* put your best face forward!

We all have a photo where we look younger, more glamorous . . . but if you send those photos, you'll likely disappoint upon the first meeting!

A recent photo where you look natural leaves room for you to impress at the first meeting!

WHAT MEN LIKE

Men are very visual and territorial.

Make sure you send a full-length photo which emphasizes your best feature. You know whether your smile, eyes, breasts, legs or rear attracts men!

Don't use a photo with anyone in it but you, especially not with the opposite sex! You want the recipient to focus only on you!

SUCCESSFUL PHOTO EXAMPLES!

ZenFemme

attracts

SpiritMovesMe

WrldTrvlr

attracts

Adventure4me

Yachtygirl

attracts

MrPositive

FlowerPower

attracts

GreenThumb

HAPPY WITH YOUR PHOTO?

NOW LOAD IT ONTO YOUR COMPUTER

SCAN YOUR PHOTO

Ask a friend with a scanner or go to a copy center or photo store to scan your photo. They'll give you a disk or CD.

Have your friend with that digital camera email the golden hour photo(s) to you.

You'll now have your photo on a DISK

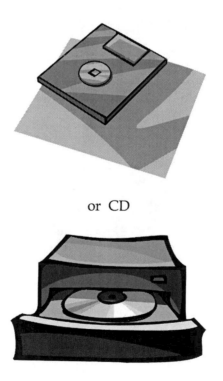

or CD

OR via EMAIL to download onto your computer.

RULE OF THUMB

<u>KEEP YOUR PHOTO</u>
<u>ON YOUR HARD DRIVE</u>

Never work directly from your disk or CD. Disks can become
lost or corrupted. Always move those files onto your hard
drive. Keep the disk or CD as your backup.

To move files from the disk or CD onto your hard drive, just
open up the picture, choose SAVE AS and save onto your
hard drive.

KEEPING IT ALL STRAIGHT!

Exactly where on your hard drive should you SAVE TO?

Remember the folders you created within the main folder named THE SEARCH?

You created a folder called PICTURES. That's where you'll save your digital picture(s).

When you're asked to UPLOAD or ATTACH your picture for your ad, you'll know exactly where it is!

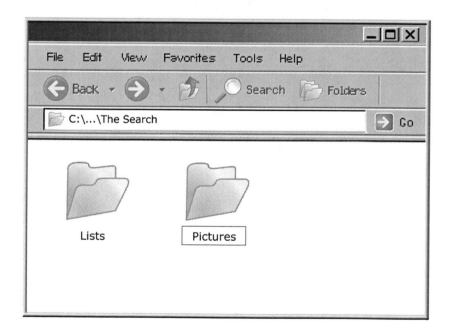

FINALLY!
CREATE AND POST YOUR AD!

BRING OUT THOSE LISTS

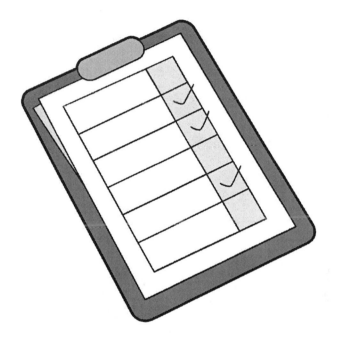

Have your lists handy as you answer the various questions from the website you've chosen.

GO TO YOUR FAVORITE SITE

The lists are guides that will reveal your innermost thoughts and desires, as well as your potential mate's.

You may not use all the info from your lists, but they're a handy resource for you to refer to in crafting your answers to the site's questions.

TOP 2 IMPROVEMENTS!

If you could only make two improvements in your ad, these would be the TOP 2:

1. Make the ad about *who you are* instead of *what you want*. To attract a man, you need to present information in this form: ***"Are you looking for what I have to offer?"***

2. Describe your true desire instead of your image of romance. Who doesn't like moonlit walks, but what is it that makes <u>you</u> special?

BIG PICTURE: ENJOY!

Don't be worried about making a mistake or creating a "bad" ad.

Remember, nothing is set in stone!

You can always revise it, or cancel the ad, create a new screen name and start again.

The point is to have fun and look forward to learning about you. Don't stress!

POST YOUR AD, THEN DOUBLE-CHECK YOUR WORK

After you've officially posted your ad, ask a friend to go to the website and check that your ad has posted correctly!

Are you in the right category?

Have you posted the right picture?

CONGRATULATIONS ON POSTING YOUR AD!

Yes, it was scary . . .

. . . but you did it!

<u>YOU MIGHT WORRY . . .</u>

Your picture and ad are out there in cyberspace and you're certain the whole world will find it immediately and laugh at you!

... BUT FEAR *NOT!*

Think back . . . when you browsed the sites, did you laugh?

And when you see women on TV who have met their husbands online, do you laugh then?

YOU ARE *NOT* BEING WATCHED, AND YOU ARE *NOT* ALONE!

The truth is, it's a very busy world. Most people are only thinking about their own lives!

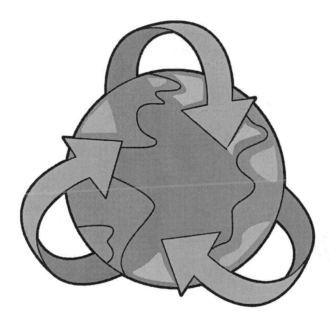

And as you saw when you browsed the dating sites, there are TONS of people placing ads on the Internet.

TAKE A BREATH!

Once your friend confirms proper posting, sit back, relax and breathe deeply. Take a bath, read a fluff magazine, have a piece of chocolate or a glass of wine and just chill for a couple days.

Think about what you've just accomplished—you're on your way to finding a healthy mate!

You'll come back refreshed and ready to continue the journey to finding your mate.

AUTHOR'S ADVICE

*I didn't want to be too picky with my first ad, so I said I'd be open
to meeting men with children, even though I don't want to be a
step-parent. When I started receiving replies from men suggesting
dates at amusement parks, I changed my ad immediately. I thought,
"Why waste their time and mine?" It feels great to be able to ask for
and receive exactly what I want!*

— Beth

Warren also loves spur-of-the-moment travel. Here we are in Kauai
for a stolen weekend away.

BEGINNER SECTION
SUMMARY

1.   Choose a computer (NOT from work) and an I.S.P.

2.   Create folders to organize your lists and pictures.

3.   Visit our website for helpful tips:
      www.justshowmewhat2do.com

4.   Check the different online dating sites to find
      your favorite.

5.   Select your favorite site by browsing with friends,
      maybe even a man similar to whom you'd like to meet.

6.   Write your LISTS (a.k.a. KEYS TO SUCCESS!)

      a.   "About the Ads"
      b.   "About Me"
      c.   "About Him"

7. Be honest with yourself. Ask a close friend/therapist to give you feedback on your lists.

8. Create a new screen name.

9. Take a new photo.

10. Move or download this photo onto your computer.

11. Compose your ad using your lists, and post it!

12. Have a good friend double-check your ad.

13. Take a break from the process and indulge yourself. You'll come back refreshed and ready for the next step!

14. Celebrate! You took the first step to finding your mate!

<u>INTERMEDIATE</u>

Screening Your Replies & Having Fun Dating

WHEN ARE YOU READY FOR THE INTERMEDIATE SECTION?

YOU JUST FINISHED THE BEGINNER SECTION

The BEGINNER SECTION taught you how to get online, then create and post your ad, but not what to do with the replies!

I'm online!

The INTERMEDIATE SECTION will introduce you to proper screening techniques to make sure you don't waste time dating the wrong guys!

INTERNET DATING VETERAN LOOKING FOR HELP

You can *start* with the INTERMEDIATE SECTION when you've created and posted an ad at least once before

AND

You've been on a few Internet dates but they didn't work out.

Therefore, you know how to create a good ad, just not how to screen the replies.

QUICK REVIEW

For the easiest path to finding your mate, make sure you've completed these items from our BEGINNER SECTION or have done them in the past on your own:

1. Go to our website for a quick orientation:

www.justshowmewhat2do.com/books

2. Keep your search organized with computer folders.

3. Fill out the "JUST <u>SHOW</u> ME . . ." lists, the essential tools to finding your mate online. You can find these lists in our BEGINNER SECTION or on our website.

4. Check out the various online dating sites and find your favorite.

5. Create a new screen name.

6. Write an ad.

7. Post your ad with a photo using our Photo "DOS & DON'TS."

NOW: THE REPLIES!

We know you're excited and anxious to get to your replies, but first you need a system to organize them on your computer for future reference.

If you're starting with the INTERMEDIATE SECTION, follow the instructions starting on page 15 in the BEGINNER SECTION to create folders for storing information on your computer.

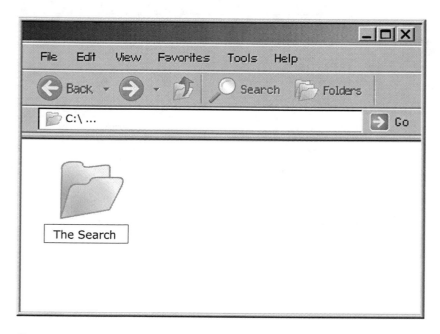

Create THE SEARCH folder as instructed.

WAIT—MORE FOLDERS!

Inside the folder you've created called THE SEARCH, create a folder and name it based upon:

1.   The name of the Online Dating Website, and
2.   The date you placed your ad.

If you're starting with this INTERMEDIATE SECTION and you placed an ad with Match.com on June 26th, 2005, THE SEARCH folder will look like this:

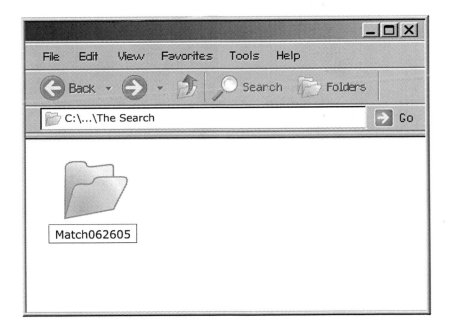

Also, create a folder called LISTS, which you'll use later in this section.

IF YOU'RE CONTINUING FROM THE BEGINNER SECTION . . .

Of course, if you started with the BEGINNER SECTION, you are creating *another* folder and THE SEARCH folder on your computer will now contain:

1.   Folders named LISTS and PICTURES, with information for your first ad.

2.   A folder named, for example, Match062605 to file information from your first ad.

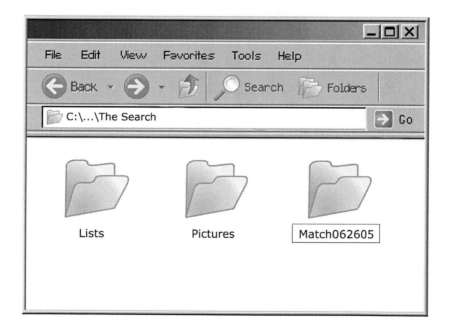

FINALLY: YOU'RE ORGANIZED!

With your folders in place, you're now prepared for the task of reviewing the replies.

As you review the replies, you'll use your new folders to keep your men organized and categorized.

A little organization goes a long way!

Free website for book purchasers!

We list more detailed instructions for items you'll need during your "FINDING YOUR MATE ONLINE" process either in previous sections or on our website:

www.justshowmewhat2do.com/books

For example, for instructions on creating folders to organize your replies, you can either refer to our BEGINNER SECTION or go online to our website!

AFTER GOLDILOCKS POSTED HER AD, SHE FOUND:

TOO FEW REPLIES,

TOO MANY REPLIES

AND JUST RIGHT!

RULE OF THUMB

There are NO numbers in this book associated with the words too *few*, too *many* and just right, because these are judgment calls based upon YOUR gut feeling.

For example, one peanut is too few for someone who loves peanuts and too many for someone allergic to them!

"Just right" is up to you!

IS THAT ALL THERE IS?

You might be depressed because you received so few replies!

This confirms your worst fears that you'll be spending the rest of your life alone!

PLAN FOR "TOO FEW REPLIES"

NUMBERS DON'T MATTER

There's no specific number associated with "too few" replies. It's what *you* feel and it will be a different amount for everyone!

Remember that the phrase "too few" can be a great thing when counting calories, weeds in your garden or pimples!

LISTS MATTER A LOT!!!

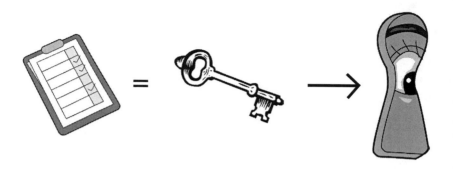

Lists contain the keys to the doors that separate you from your mate.

If you feel you received too few replies,
then return to the BEGINNER SECTION and:

1.   Revise your lists.

2.   Revise your ad.

3.   Revise your photo.

4.   Revise your dating screen name.

DON'T TRY THIS ALONE

Add some fresh perspective. Call in a close friend or relative for objective feedback to help you be honest about your revisions.

A REVISED AD MEANS A NEW FOLDER

Don't forget—you'll need a new folder for your revised ad!

Use the same rules for adding and naming folders we've used in the past for consistency.

In the example below, you created a revised ad on July 22, 2005.

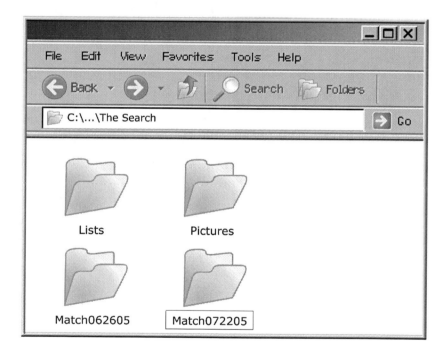

AUTHOR'S ADVICE

Only 1 guy replied to the first ad I posted—and he lived across the country! I went back and reviewed my lists and then revised my ad. I also changed my photo—the first photo showed me all bundled up on a winter hike . . . and I only occasionally hike! It was just a photo a friend sent to me in digital format. This time, I still chose a casual shot, but one that showed me rollerblading, one of my favorite sports, and showed off my figure— my best feature! The new ad got plenty of replies!

—Karin

A year after we met, we tried working together! Here we are in Italy while touring with singer Cassandra Wilson.

HERE COME THE REPLIES!

You might be panicking because you've received a lot of replies . . .

And you might actually have to go out on one of those dates you've been whining about never having!

PLAN FOR "TOO MANY REPLIES"

WHEN TOO MUCH IS OVERLOAD

QUESTION: How do you know if you've gotten "too many" replies?

ANSWER: If you feel that there's no way you'll be able to juggle dating all those guys . . .

TO THE RESCUE

Don't worry about juggling.

Our "Too Many Replies Plan" will save you from the *"will never work"* ads and only keep the *"good possibility"* ads before you actually plan a date with anyone.

TIME FOR NATURAL SELECTION

Go back to your lists. Print and review the lists

1.　　"ABOUT ME"

and

2.　　"ABOUT HIM"

Keep these at your side as you look through your replies.
Compare each guy to what you've put in your lists . . . *is he a match?*

BE DISCRIMINATING

As you sort through the many replies, DELETE the obvious *"WILL NEVER WORK* choices, which include . . .

1. Any reply without a photo (no matter how great he *sounds* in his email!). He's not serious about this online dating process!

2. Any "form" reply sent to anything female—they'll be obvious.

3. Reject those that YOU KNOW will never work. Use the "ABOUT ME" list you've got at your side or, if you started in the INTERMEDIATE SECTION, answer the question on the following page.

IMPROVE YOUR ODDS

Answer this question about your previous dates to help you determine what replies *"WILL NEVER WORK."*

In my failed relationships, the consistent problems in the *men* **I pick are:** _____.

This doesn't imply the men are *failures* . . . You can be dating Prince Charmings that don't work for you because, for example, they don't want children and you do.

The relationship *failed* because you continued to date Prince Charming, hoping he'd change his mind!

THE DEFINITION OF INSANITY

One definition of insanity is *doing the same thing over and over again expecting a different result.*

Answer this question about yourself so you don't keep making the same mistakes in your relationships and expect a positive result!

So if you have many failed relationships with men struggling to be an actor, musician, etc. with no desire to start a family—DELETE THOSE REPLIES!

RULE OF THUMB

THE IMPORTANCE OF FAITH

The most important "how-to" of this book is having the faith that you will find your mate.

We're going to ask you to eliminate some otherwise eligible men simply because they don't meet your criteria based upon your "ABOUT HIM" list.

The Rule of Thumb for every success story in every aspect of life—business, adventure, personal triumph—is faith.

Believe that you will find your mate and it will happen! Our book helps you make it happen more easily and quickly.

RELAX . . .
THIS IS THE FUN PART

We know it seems tedious, but savor these moments. Remember, once you're married, you'll never go on a first date again.

WHEN YOU'RE GOLDILOCKS THE REPLIES FEEL "JUST RIGHT"

BECOMING GOLDILOCKS

There are many ways to become Goldilocks where the replies feel "just right."

1. "Too Few" replies became Goldilocks by returning to the BEGINNING SECTION and revising her lists, ad, photo and dating screen name.

2. "Too Many" replies became Goldilocks by deleting the obvious replies that won't work.

3. You felt the number of replies were "Just Right," and you're starting here.

WWW

Free website for book purchasers!

How do you find your mate within all these replies?

You've already described your future mate in your "About Him" list.

Time to pull it out again!

As always, you can download this form from our website . . .

www.justshowmewhat2do.com/books

. . . or copy it from the next 2 pages.

LIST #3: "ABOUT HIM"

(TAKE YOUR TIME FILLING THIS OUT! IF YOU NEED MORE SPACE, COPY AND PASTE ADDITIONAL LINES. THE MORE YOU OUTLINE HERE, THE MORE YOU FINE-TUNE YOUR SEARCH FOR YOUR MATE!)

1. I am looking for a partner for
    a. Dating only. Someone to have fun with on weekends. I'm not ready for a serious relationship.
    b. Marriage but no children.
    c. Marriage and _____(#) of children.

2. In a letter to my best friend, where I hold nothing back, I describe him as _____
_____.

3. On a typical weekend, we really enjoy doing _____ on a Friday night, then _____ on a Saturday, then _____ on a Sunday.

4. His looks remind me of _____.

5. He's _____ years old.

6. As far as health, he's _____.

7. His spiritual/religious beliefs are _____.

8. He wants _____ kids.

9. He already has _____ kids.

10. He's been married _____ times.

11. His career is _____.

12. His attitude about money is _____.

13. His attitude toward his family is _____.

14. He treats me _____.

15. When I tell him I'd like to spend a romantic evening, we do
_____.

16. His politics are _____.

17. He treats female friends, co-workers and acquaintances like
_____.

18. I'm proud to have him as my boyfriend when _____
_____.

19. My parents like him because _____.

20. My siblings like him because _____.

21. My friends like him because _____.

22. I love him because _____
_____.

**ONCE YOU FINISH FILLING OUT THIS LIST,
SAVE IT IN YOUR "LISTS" FOLDER
THAT IS WITHIN "THE SEARCH" FOLDER.**

YES OR NO

Let's start out simply.

Review each email response and compare it to your "ABOUT HIM" list.

You'll feel either:

1. YES! I want to know more.

2. NO, I'm not interested.

This is how you'll organize your first set of email responses.

SO MANY MEN . . .

Create folders for your 2 GROUPS:

1.   The KNOW MORE folder

2.   The NO MORE folder

If you're organizing responses to your Match.com June 26th ad, your computer screen should look like this:

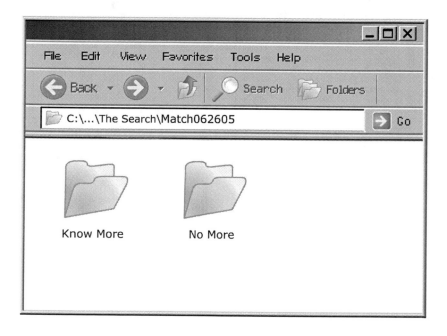

NAME YOUR "KNOW MORES"

For the "KNOW MORE" replies, create a folder for each man using his screen name.

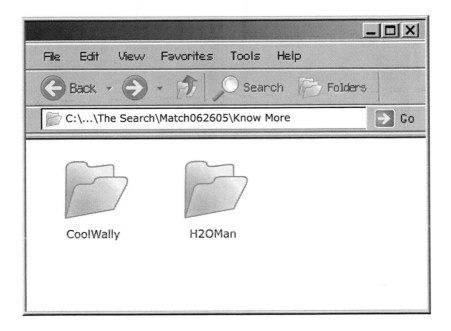

When you click on the KNOW MORE folder, your screen will look like the above, with many folders of each man!

SIMPLIFY YOUR "NO MORES"

For the "NO MORE" replies, just save the email in the NO MORE folder.

You don't need to create individual folders for each man like you did in the KNOW MORE folder.

No need to waste time organizing replies from men who aren't right for you.

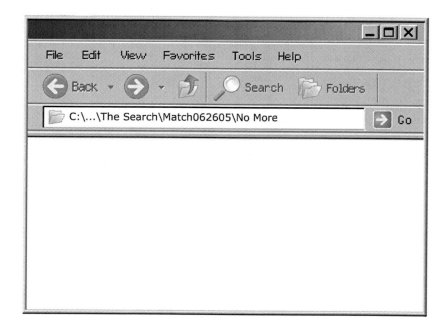

TAKE A BREATH!

If your brain feels fried after organizing and creating folders, take a break and take a breath!

Do something fun, then come back to the computer refreshed.

We want you to be excited about sifting through the responses to find your mate, not overwhelmed by the process!

THE ACCOMPLISHMENTS!

If you did take a break, good for you for knowing your limit! Either way, here's what you've accomplished so far:

1.   Regardless of how you started, you became Goldilocks, and your number of replies felt just right.

2.   You read the emails and listened to your gut reaction which said either "Yes, I want to KNOW MORE" or "No, I'm not interested, so NO MORE."

3.   You created individual folders within the KNOW MORE folder for each man based upon his screen name.

4.   You filed all the NO emails together in the NO MORE folder since there's no need to categorize them by name.

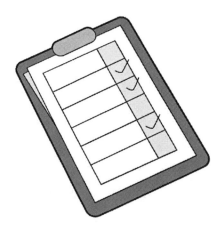

YOUR SECRET WEAPON: THE SECRET SCREENER!

FINDING GREAT CHEMISTRY

Now that we've figured out which men *might be* right, let's take a closer look at the men in the KNOW MORE folder using our SECRET SCREENER!

SECRET WHAT?

Secret Screener is our TOOL to shape your first email answer to him to help you learn information important to you about the KNOW MORES.

It's five questions you'd like to know about a man before a date, but phrased in a way that won't turn men off!

You should pick issues that are important to you and could impact whether you'd accept a first date.

ISN'T HONESTY THE BEST POLICY?

Of course! The word secret refers to subtly asking about significant dating issues—the kinds of topics most men don't offer in emails, but will respond to if asked properly.

CREATE YOUR SECRET SCREENER

What are the TOP 5 QUESTIONS you want to know about a man before going on a date?

For example:

1. Does he have a profession and not just a job?

2. Did he go to college and, if so, did he get his degree?

3. Is he active or a couch potato?

4. What is his religion?

5. Does he have kids?

SORT WITH YOUR SECRET SCREENER

Remember how you sorted through all the email responses with your "ABOUT HIM" list?

This is the same process!

1.   Review each email response in your
        "KNOW MORE" folder.

2.   Did his reply answer your 5 questions
        in your SECRET SCREENER?

Hint: *The answer is probably no!*

REALITY CHECK

Most men aren't going to offer a whole lot of information in their response.

We accept that men and women are very different, yin and yang, so we're going to have to pose our SECRET SCREENER questions in our reply to the men!

In the next column, we give you an example of an email reply using the SECRET SCREENER from page 120.

EMAIL USING YOUR SECRET SCREENER

Hi Jackson,

Thanks for your reply.   I really liked your picture. You remind me of a guy I had a crush on in college.   Where'd you go to school *(RE: 2)?*

I'd love to get together, but I have a big deadline in two weeks, so could we trade emails until then? I'm in advertising, so my hours ebb and flow. Do you have regular hours? What business are you in *(RE: 1)?*

Are you available to meet for weekend brunch? Sundays I go to the Unitarian church, but am open to all religions. Do you belong to a church *(RE: 4)?*

I'm also open to sharing some of your favorite activities—that is if I can! What do you like to do on weekends *(RE: 3&5)?*

HELPFUL HINT

In this initial stage of responding, you can use pretty much the same reply to all the men.

Don't agonize about creating a perfect reply! Just make sure you haven't asked a question they've already answered, like what they do for a living or their religion.

If you keep your first response short and complimentary—two things that men love—you're sure to receive a reply and learn some more about the man.

Free website for book purchasers!

Need help figuring out questions for your

SECRET SCREENER?

You can download a list of our sample SECRET SCREENER questions from our website:

www.justshowmewhat2do.com/books

AUTHOR'S ADVICE

Ninety percent of the replies to my email said something like, "You sound great! Call me." It took a lot of emails, calls and dates to find out the important things about the men I wanted to know, and I wasn't always comfortable asking upfront. Once I created my own SECRET SCREENER, I was able to find out in one email what it would have taken three dates to ask outright.

—Beth

My SECRET SCREENER helped me find a man who loves to cook and lets me pour the wine.

THE PHONE GAME

Throughout the INTERMEDIATE section, we've concentrated on using email for correspondence because:

1.   We tend to be bolder and more honest when we're not face to face.

2.   Writing allows us to gather our thoughts.

3.   Emails feel safer than giving out our phone number.

Once you've used email to narrow the crowd, you'll still want to screen by phone before meeting in person.

Telephone screening is great because you get a feel whether there's chemistry . . . or not.

SCREENING SAFELY BY PHONE

Screen a phone conversation as you would an email.

Make a LIST of what you want to know about this person and subtly incorporate these questions into your conversation.

If you don't feel good about his response, HANG UP AND MOVE ON!

Worried about using your home or cell phone in case the recipient has caller ID?

Call your carrier to make sure that both your home and cell numbers are "blocked."   This may be an extra charge. Test this out with a friend first who has caller ID.

Now you can feel safe in finding out if there's still the chemistry you shared in your emails.

HAVING FUN DATING!

BE CAREFUL
WHAT YOU WISH FOR . . .

By sorting through all your replies and emailing using your
SECRET SCREENER . . . you've found quite a few men with
whom you feel you could have some chemistry.

WHAT NOW?

YOU GO ON A LOT OF DATES!

Just remember . . . *practice makes perfect!* You've got to hit millions of tennis balls before you can serve an ace at Wimbledon.

And you may date many men before you receive your online trophy—finding your mate!

JUGGLING MULTIPLE DATES?

You'll probably be excited, nervous and second guessing yourself all at the same time!

All change brings about anxiety, even great changes like a trip to Paris . . . or finding your husband!

THE UPSIDE OF JUGGLING:

Dating is like a job interview!

Even if you really want to work at NBC, you still take the interview at CBS, because you just never know!

Dating is like shoe shopping!

When you're shopping for shoes for a wedding, you go to all the shoe stores in the mall, instead of depending on finding the perfect pair at Bloomingdale's.

Dating is like multi-tasking!

You don't do one thing at a time, do you? No! You talk to your mother on the phone while you surf the net on your laptop as you watch television.

SCHEDULING MULTIPLE DATES:

Now that we've determined that multiple dates are a good thing, let's do it the easy way!

1.   Email your replies in a timely manner—within a couple days—even if you can't meet that person right away.

You want to establish that you're a polite, responsible, potential mate.

2. Keep the level of involvement equal among the dates: Don't meet one man for coffee, then spend all day at the beach with another.

You need an even playing field for comparison.

3. If it doesn't feel right, don't force it. Don't go out on second or third dates because he's a "nice guy"—if you don't feel that spark, don't waste your time.

You don't have to start dating right away. Use email and phone calls to get enough information about each guy to know whether he sounds like a good match.

Take at least two weeks emailing and calling back and forth, screening and evaluating his personality and character before scheduling your first date.

DATING DOS & DON'TS!

1. *Do* relax and **have fun** . . . don't think too hard on the date about whether or not this person is "the one."

2. *Don't* wait till you've had a first date with everyone before you have a second date with someone you liked!

3.   ***Do*** take some time for introspection every couple weeks. Review all of the emails of the people that you really like and review the candidates—how do they match up to your lists?

4.   ***Don't*** talk yourself into a second date if you have any hesitation at all.

AUTHOR'S ADVICE

After emailing several weeks, I went out with "Robert." While he didn't "wow" me, he was a nice guy and seemed like a good person. I thought I should give him another chance, and accepted 2 more dates with him. After the 3rd date, I knew in my heart he wasn't for me, and we parted ways. I realized that nothing changed between the 1st and 3rd dates, so why did I waste time just because he was a "nice guy"?

I never did again.

—Karin

I wanted a mate who loved island vacations also! Here we are under a waterfall on the "Road to Hana" in Hawaii. We got engaged a couple days later!

SAFETY NOTES

Internet dating is no more or less safe than any other type of dating. Here are some safety tips for every situation!

1. Never go out with someone if something just doesn't seem right!

   Through several weeks of emails, you should be able to verify at least his work phone number.

2. If you call from your home and/or cell phone, make sure your number is blocked and refuses all blocked calls. Call your carrier for details.

3.   Always meet in a public place.

"I do love hiking but I'd be more comfortable meeting our first time for a latte at a coffee shop."

4.   Arrange your own transportation to and from the date.

5.   Let your date know you're giving his name and where you'll be to a friend in case of emergency.

"Danny, I left our names and the number of this restaurant with my sister in case of an emergency. Sometimes my cell phone doesn't get great coverage inside."

6.   Use your friends for some added perspective. If you
        have any doubts about a guy, show them your ad and
        his responses, then see what they think.

7.   Ask a friend to expect your call at the end of the date
        when you've returned home safely. They should know
        where you're meeting and your date's contact info.

8.   Better yet, meet on a double-date! Bring another
        couple whose instincts you trust. If the date goes well,
        you can arrange a signal for them to leave after one
        drink or cup of coffee!

        *"My friends are going to be in the area and would like to join
        us for a drink. Is this okay with you?"*

9.　　　Google him!

Type his name and some basic information into a search engine like www.google.com.

"John Brown" "ski instructor"

Note: Put quotes around a group of words to find them together instead of separately like *"John and his brown dog . . ."* when you mean *"John Brown."*

You'd be surprised what the Internet has on individuals, including yourself!

10.　　　Email his name, phone number and any other details he's responded to your screening, to at least 2 friends.

<u>THIS IS NOT A TEST!</u>

The good news about dating: There are no right or wrong answers!

You're not going to be graded, you're not going to be judged, you're not going to fail.

Release all expectations and remove the pressure from yourself!

POSITIVE ATTRACTS POSITIVE

Being excited about dating, whether or not you meet "the one" right away, gives you a positive vibe that makes you more attractive.

This vibe will be noticeable wherever you go, so remember to keep a positive attitude on your dates and during the entire process.

If you have a less than perfect experience, laugh about it! These will be the stories you share with others when recounting the work it took to meet your mate.

TAKE A BREATH!

Everything in moderation is great advice!

Dating is like chocolate, fine wine and shopping. Know when to take a break or you'll end up sick, drunk and broke!

Since everyone is different, there are no numbers or time references to guide you . . . just follow your instinct.

Take a breath when you feel you need time for yourself and use this time for reflection and to review your lists.

You'll start the adventure again refreshed and focused!

AUTHOR'S ADVICE

I was having a great time dating and it really raised my self-esteem.
I realized I got off track, however, when I continued accepting dates
with men who didn't excite me. The holidays were approaching, so I
decided to take a break. It was a great time to re-evaluate what I was
looking for in a man. On my return, I had a new focus, and shortly
thereafter, I met my husband.

—Beth

Warren has his captain's license, and sailing is one of our favorite
sports. Sydney Harbour, Australia.

INTERMEDIATE SECTION SUMMARY

1. Post your ad and wait for replies.   Be excited!

2. If "TOO FEW REPLIES," go back to the Beginning Section and:

   (a) revise your lists
   (b) revise your ad
   (c) revise your photo
   (d) revise your dating screen name

   Remember: a new ad requires a new folder!

3. If "TOO MANY REPLIES," reject the obvious:

   (a) no photos
   (b) form email
   (c) will never work

4. Pull out or fill out your "ABOUT HIM" list.   Compare the email replies to this list and sort into two groups:

   (a) Know More
   (b) No More

5.   Create folders for the KNOW MORE'S and the NO MORE'S.

6.   Within the KNOW MORE folder, create individual folders for each man and name it according to his screen name.

7.   No need to sort individually the NO MORE'S. Just move them into the folder.

8.   Create the TOP 5 QUESTIONS you'd like to know about a man that he probably won't offer to tell you. This is your SECRET SCREENER!

9.   Write your first reply incorporating your SECRET SCREENER questions in a subtle way. Keep it short and flattering!

10.   Schedule multiple dates easily with these helpful tips:

      (a) Email back in a timely manner even if you can't meet right away.

      (b) Screen by phone for chemistry.

      (c) Keep the playing field level. Meet everyone for coffee or everyone for lunch, etc.

      (d) Don't go out with someone you know isn't right just because he's a nice guy.

11.   Follow our Dating DOS & DON'TS.

12.   Incorporate our SAFETY NOTES into your dates.

13.   Have fun dating. Be positive and you'll glow!

SECTION THREE

ADVANCED

Finding & Marrying Your Mate

WHEN ARE YOU READY FOR THE ADVANCED SECTION?

YOU JUST FINISHED THE INTERMEDIATE SECTION

The INTERMEDIATE SECTION gave you a busy social calendar, but not your mate!

The ADVANCED SECTION will give you the tools to focus on the prize—meeting your mate online!

20 DATES

You can *start* with the ADVANCED SECTION when . . .

1.   You've gone on at least 20 Internet dates AND/OR

2.   You've been in an Internet relationship for at least 6 months that was ended by either party.

KEEPING IT REAL!

Proceeding to the ADVANCED SECTION *before* you're ready is like going shoe shopping at a great outlet mall during their big clearance sale . . .

and forgetting your purse!

Why subject yourself to this exercise in frustration?

THE BEST PLACE TO START!

Starting at the BEGINNER or INTERMEDIATE SECTIONS *when* they're the right places for you is like learning that sex burns more calories than running.

Fun and good for you!

NOW YOU'RE READY ... LET'S GO

You're almost at the Winner's Circle . . .

Keep your focus and your eyes on the prize.

QUICK REVIEW

For the easiest path to finding your mate, make sure you've completed these items from our BEGINNER and INTERMEDIATE sections or have done them in the past on your own:

1. Go to our website for a quick orientation:

www.justshowmewhat2do.com/books

2. Keep your search organized with individual computer folders.

3. Fill out the "JUST <u>SHOW</u> ME . . . " lists, the essential tools to finding your mate online. You can find these lists in our BEGINNER SECTION pages 37, 45, and 49–50 or go to our website to download.

QUICK REVIEW (CONT'D)

4. Check out the various online dating sites and find
    your favorite.

5. Create a new screen name.

6. Write an ad.

7. Post your ad with a photo.

8. Wait for replies and be excited!

9. "TOO FEW REPLIES?" Revise your lists, ad, photo
    and screen name.

10. "TOO MANY REPLIES?" Reject form emails, no
    photos, incompatible men.

QUICK REVIEW (CONT'D)

11.   Sort your replies into two computer folders, "KNOW MORE" and "NO MORE."

12.   Within the KNOW MORE folder, create individual folders for each man and name it according to his screen name.   The NO MORE'S can all go in one folder.

13.   Create the top 5 questions you'd like to know about a man that he probably won't offer to tell you. This is your SECRET SCREENER!

14.   Write your first reply incorporating your SECRET SCREENER questions in a subtle way.   Keep it short and flattering!

15.   Schedule multiple dates and HAVE FUN DATING!

I'M AN EXPERT AT DATING . . .
WHEN CAN I STOP?

RE-EXAMINE THE PROCESS

The ADVANCED SECTION takes the experiences from
your last Internet dating attempt and helps you re-examine
the process:

*What changes should you make in Online Dating
to make it your last date?*

CREATE AN "ADVANCED AD"

The first change is to create an "ADVANCED AD."

The purpose of the ADVANCED AD is to get real, get clear and get focused right now on exactly who you are and what you want.

To assist in the creation, you'll come up with what we call . . .

THE "TOP 3"

THE "TOP 3"

Write down your reactions to your last 20 Internet dates or
Internet relationship:

- Top 3 **"I really liked . . . "**
- Top 3 **"I really hated . . . "**
- Top 3 **"I wish . . . "**
- Top 3 **"Uh oh . . . "**

For a handy form, go to our website:

www.justshowmewhat2do.com/books

TOP 3 "I REALLY LIKED . . ."

You love museums, so naturally you figured fellow museum-lovers would be your passion.

Imagine your surprise when you discovered that nature lovers really turn you on.

Who knew that you *really liked* flannel wearing, he-men campers who both catch and cook the dinner!

TOP 3 "I REALLY HATED . . ."

Don't **judge** your dislikes, just recognize them!

Forget what your mother or your therapist might say!

If you *really hated* that his jokes seemed racist, or even that he didn't know a Merlot from a Cabernet, write it down!

TOP 3 "I WISH . . ."

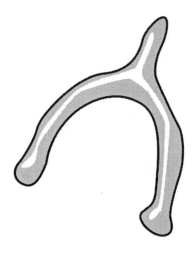

By now you've probably dated a great guy and said to yourself, "*I wish* he was Jewish; *I wish* he didn't travel for work; *I wish* he wanted kids; *I wish* he didn't already have kids . . . "

This isn't the time to be politically correct! If you prefer Jewish over Christian . . . a man who wants kids . . . makes more money, that's your heart speaking, so listen.

TOP 3 "UH OH . . ."

If it bothers you when a man spends his weekends with his kids or . . . watches sports all afternoon or . . . doesn't get along with his family, etc., it doesn't make him a bad person, he just might not be the person for you!

If you've given it a good try but think *"uh oh"* when he turns on the TV Saturday afternoons, then the football fanatic just might be meant for someone else.

AUTHOR'S ADVICE

Worth the effort! Three years after we met, we got married on Captiva Island, Florida.

I had high hopes when I started my journey online to find my mate, especially when my friend met her husband in just months! My process, however, took several years. I would grow discouraged, pull my ads, and feel sorry for myself. I stuck with it and had the faith to continue all the way, learning lessons which became our Advanced Section. For my efforts, I was rewarded with a great man!

—Karin

REVIEW YOUR PREVIOUS AD

Compare your earlier ad to:

1.   Your TOP 3 **"I wish . . . "**
2.   Your TOP 3 **"I really liked . . . "**

Look for the patterns! You'll probably see a lot of things you want to change, add to, etc.

Spontaneous, athletic, attractive!

"I love a man with a great sense of humor who loves to travel!
I hope you like moonlit walks, museums and movies. If you
don't know how to, I'll teach you to rollerblade and sail—two
of my passions.

I have a dog, no kids, but I do want to settle down and have
kids. You live within 30 miles from (my area).

This picture tells a lot about me: playful, adventurous, fun.
This is a couch in London's Sanderson Hotel. I love to travel
and I hope you do, too."

PREVIOUS AD

In your previous ad, you asked for the following:

What I want in a man:

- He has a great sense of humor
- He wants to get married & have kids
- He loves to travel

You also listed your images of romance as:

- Moonlit walks
- Going to museums
- Going to movies

YOUR NEW TOP 3

Based upon what you've learned in creating your TOP 3, here's an example of your new desires. Then we'll describe how to incorporate them into your new "ADVANCED AD!"

TOP 3: **"I wish . . . "**

- He doesn't already have kids
- He wants to get married & have kids
- He loves sailing or wants to learn

TOP 3: **"I really liked . . . "**

- He loved wine
- He could fix anything
- He got along great with his family

TOP 2 IMPROVEMENTS

In our BEGINNER SECTION, we listed the top 2 ways women can improve their ads. These bear repeating:

1. Make the ad about *who you are* instead of *what you want.* To attract a man, you need to present information in this form: **"Are you looking for what I have to offer?"**

2. Describe your true desire instead of your image of romance. Just about everybody likes moonlit walks, but what is it that makes *you* special?

PUTTING IT ALL TOGETHER

Rewrite your ad with these simple rules:

1.   Make your TOP 3 "I wish" into what you have to offer.

Instead of *"I want kids . . . "* you would pose the question *"do you desire someone to create a great life and family together?"*

2.   When you describe images of romance, list those items you *really* do, not what you wish you did!

Think about your past several weekends as opposed to in the past year for clues to what you like to do and what types of activities are important to you.

CREATE YOUR "ADVANCED" AD!

SUCCESSFUL AD REVISED
(revisions in *italics*)

Spontaneous, athletic, attractive —
likes to please mate.

"Do you have a great social life with many friends, but you're looking to meet someone who wants to create a life and family together?

I have a lot to offer—rollerblading and sailing are two of my passions.   I also like to share my partner's passions.

This picture tells a lot about me: playful, adventurous, fun. This is a couch in the Sanderson Hotel in London."

SUCCESSFUL AD REVISED (CONT'D)

(revisions in *italics*)

"My previous boyfriend told me I'm a great traveling partner, adaptive and open to new experiences. Unfortunately, he already had his children, and I didn't want to be a stepmom, so we parted good friends.

If you desire a woman who appreciates great wine, sailing, and your handyman skills, let's email!

Please live within 30 miles from (my area).

Looking forward to your reply."

RULE OF THUMB

THE MORE THE MERRIER

Now that you have an awesome ad describing what you really know about yourself and what's important to you, get it out there!

Post the ad on a second online dating site.

Remember that you can sign up for introductory offers on a lot of sites.

If you like the responses you receive, you can sign up for a longer time.

AUTHOR'S ADVICE

When people hear that I married the 5th man I met online, they always ask me what I said in my ad to attract him. It's not really what I said, it's how I said it. My ad talked about me—where I came from, who I am, and where I'm going. No gimmicks, no excuses, no cliches. My best advice is never to oversell. Be yourself in your ad. That's what will attract the man you're looking for. Be diligent in knowing who you are and what you're looking for, apply that to your screening and only meet those who pass all the tests. Follow those simple steps, and you'll have people asking what you said in your ad to attract YOUR husband!

—Beth

Early in our dating years . . . note the glow of happiness when you finally find your mate!

FILING REFRESHER

You'll need NEW files for your advanced ad!

If you're starting with the ADVANCED SECTION, go to page 86 to learn what files to create.

If you're continuing from the INTERMEDIATE SECTION, you'll know that if you placed your advanced ad on October 15th on J-Date, the next step is to:

Create a folder called JDATE101505 then two more folders inside for Mr.'s KNOW MORE and Mr.'s NO MORE.

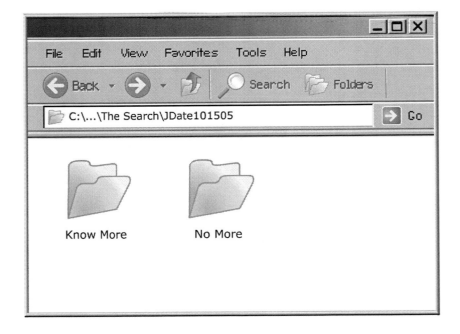

FILING REFRESHER

Within the KNOW MORE folder, create individual folders for each man using their screen names.

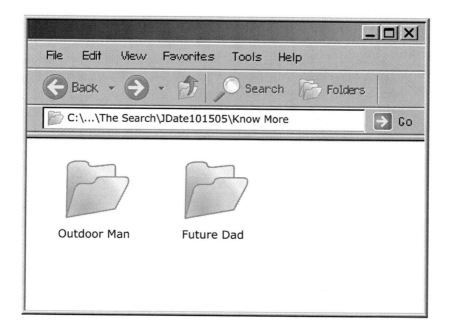

You don't need individual folders for Mr.'s NO MORE.

A WORD OF CAUTION

Here's the disclaimer, the fine print, the legalese:

You're going to be going on fewer dates and getting fewer replies.

WHEN LESS IS MORE

Just when you've been filling your Friday and Saturday nights with all kinds of activities, you're going to find yourself slowing down.

That's okay, because . . .

AND THE WINNER IS:

. . . your goal is to have *no more dates,* isn't it?

QUALITY OVER QUANTITY

Now quality over quantity is the objective!

DOUBLE-CHECK YOUR WORK

Ask a friend to go to the website and check that your ad has posted correctly!

- Are you in the right category?

- Have you uploaded the right picture?

Go celebrate!

TAKE A BREATH!

Great work! When you've completed the steps below, take a breath and take a break. Indulge in something you enjoy, so you'll come back refreshed!

1. You created your TOP 3'S.

2. You revised your ad with the TOP 3'S *"I really liked . . ."* and *"I wish . . . "*

3. You placed your new "ADVANCED AD."

4. You filed these new replies in a new folder you've created for your "ADVANCED AD."

TYPE A's . . .
WE KNOW YOUR TRICKS!

Relaxing and refreshing both your body and mind is as important as any other step in this book.

So don't skip the easy step of chilling in the bath with a favorite magazine or going on a sunset hike!

Just imagine yourself relaxing in the future with your mate!

DETOURS IN THE PATH OF ENLIGHTENMENT

Maybe you found love online in the past and thought you had the real thing, but things didn't work out.

How can you avoid the same mistake?

MAKING SURE IT'S THE "REAL THING"

SECRET WEAPONS

Your lists are your secret weapons!

Making lists is like having your best friend AND a time management expert with you on all your dates.

YOUR JOURNEY

In the **BEGINNER SECTION**, your lists explored your self image and your desires.

In the **INTERMEDIATE SECTION**, your lists identified what you wanted in a man and who you might have chemistry with.

And now, in the **ADVANCED SECTION**, your lists will focus on attracting your true partner.

THE ENVELOPE PLEASE ...

How can you turn your Documentary into Best Picture?

THE WRITE STUFF

The award comes from writing your thoughts about each date.

It doesn't matter whether you write your list that night or the next morning . . . just do it!

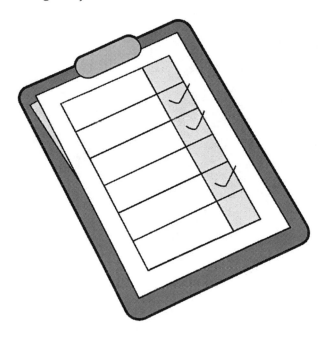

On the next page, we're providing you with a "DATE RECAP" for each date.

To download a form, go to our website:

www.justshowmewhat2do.com/books

WRITING A "DATE RECAP" AFTER EACH DATE

DATE RECAP

Write the following after each date:

1. What worked:

2. What didn't work:

3. I really liked:

4. I really hated:

5. I wish:

6. I felt "uh oh" when:

7. Learned about myself:

8. Feelings about this date:

9. Willing to see him again?

DON'T WORRY, BE HAPPY!

Don't worry if you don't have notes for all nine!

The objective is to eventually find a partner with <u>few</u>
"Uh oh . . . " or *"I wish.."*

BUT <u>many</u> *"I really liked . . . "*

No longer will you date someone about whom you would say
"I really hated . . . "

. . . NO MATTER WHAT *OTHER* GREAT QUALITIES THEY POSSESS!

<u>OF COURSE, BE SENSIBLE</u>

Are the issues you hate *significant* issues?

1.   If they eliminate everyone, like *"I hate when he watches sports,"* this should probably not count as a significant issue. Most men like sports.

2.   Get a married friend's feedback. Most married girlfriends want to help you find a mate. They'll give you the 411 as to whether or not you're being sensible.

PRACTICE TIME IS OVER!

You're at the point where you don't need to practice dating a great guy who, for example, doesn't want kids if you do!

You've gone on enough dates now to know exactly what you want.

FOCUS, FOCUS, FOCUS!

EXCEPTIONAL 3

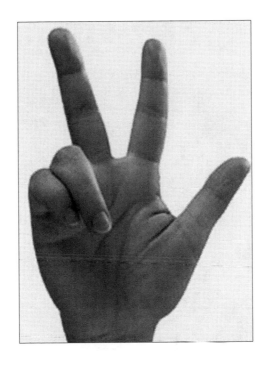

We're going to limit you to the number of men you can date and correspond with at one time.

Pick 3 EXCEPTIONAL MEN and then pull your ad!

All your concentration is going to be on these 3 men without the pressure of dealing with other responses!

WHAT A STRANGE TRIP IT'S BEEN!

You probably didn't know as much about yourself when you bought this book as you do now.

Your *"I really liked . . . "* and *"Uh oh . . . "* changed from what you thought you wanted.

OLYMPIC MOMENT

You've been practicing for years . . . now you're in the Olympics going for the gold.

Your DATE RECAPS will clearly reveal whether or not to go on another date.

The following is an example of a First DATE RECAP:

"DATE #1 RECAP WITH STEVE"
(GivePeaceAChance@____.com)

1.   What worked: *Easy conversation*
2.   What didn't work: n/a
3.   I really liked: *Very active with local charities & Habitat for Humanity*
4.   I really hated: n/a
5.   I wish: n/a
6.   I felt "uh-oh": *Rough, calloused hands*
7.   Learned about myself: *Don't judge too much by the screen name!*
8.   Feelings about this date: *I was a little worried about his screen name—would he be too crunchy granola for me? But I was really turned on by all the charitable work he does. He went to an Ivy League school, obviously has good manners and breeding and knows wine, but he chose to design & build custom furniture rather than be a lawyer, etc.*
9.   Willing to see him again? **YES!**

HIDDEN WARNING SIGNS

THE GOOD NEWS: You've done amazing work in figuring out exactly what you want in a partner and sorting through these potential mates via email.

THE BAD NEWS: Your potential mates don't have this book, so they may not be as clear as you on what they want.

You may discover some hidden warning signs only in person!

RULE OF THUMB

Despite your best efforts, if certain WARNING SIGNS show up on the first date, move on!

Concentrate on #2 and #3 of your EXCEPTIONAL 3.

These warning signs are significant *"I wish . . . "* or *"I hated . . . "*

For a reminder on what "significant" might include, review our HELPFUL HINT on page 195.

HOW MANY DATES BEFORE YOU KNOW?

MAGIC NUMBER 6

You've gone on 6 dates with a wonderful man. You think he's the one . . . but you've thought that before!

How can you tell he's a potential mate, not a future disappointment? Review your 6 DATE RECAPS!

The goal is to have no more *"I wish . . . "* or *"I hated."* Those are deal breakers.

You should have many more *"I really liked."* This is the wooing period!

There will always be some *"Uh oh . . . "* as no one's perfect.

EYE ON THE PRIZE!

If none of your EXCEPTIONAL 3 was "the one," don't despair. You finally have your eye on the prize!

You're more in tune with these ADVANCED SECTION dates than you ever felt before.

Don't be disappointed—*okay, maybe just a bit!* Instead, take what you've learned from your EXCEPTIONAL 3 and place your ad again or tweak it slightly.

THE SECOND LAP

Place the same ad again without any changes, unless you've made an obvious about-face in your desires.

By now you're on the right track, it just takes a few more laps.

So you'll start again from page 197, "EXCEPTIONAL 3."

If you want to change something in your TOP 3, then start again from page 163.

ON THE OTHER HAND . . . CONGRATULATIONS!

You and Steve have a great and healthy relationship!

Now you can put away this book—*we'll miss you!*—and concentrate on building the relationship.

Of course, you can't know anyone after 6 dates, but if there are no *"I wish . . . "* or *"I hated,"* plenty of *"I really liked,"* and you've added one more *"Uh oh . . . "* that many of us share—*his mother thinks no one's good enough for her son*—then Steve is definitely worth pursuing!

CELEBRATE THE WOMAN YOU'VE BECOME!

Look in the mirror and you'll see a different person than when you first started this book, whatever section you started with.

You are a more confident woman because you know exactly what you want and are willing to work hard to achieve your goals.

You're proud of placing personal ads and you're probably an inspiration to other women who want to find their mate but aren't sure what to do.

Celebrate the woman you've become!

TAKE A BREATH!

Continue to balance your accomplishments with "me time" to reflect upon these achievements.

This book wasn't just about helping you find your mate online; It guided you in setting your goals, it encouraged you with motivation and it reminded you to TAKE A BREATH every so often to keep you balanced.

AUTHOR'S ADVICE

It was only after writing all the lists, the TOP 3'S, and our SECRET SCREENERS that we realized why we hadn't had success in relationships before . . . We didn't know ourselves! We dated men we thought we should like instead of what really made us happy. Once we figured out ourselves, there seemed to be great, available men everywhere, when just months earlier we couldn't find anyone we liked to date!

—Karin and Beth

Warren & Beth celebrating three years of marriage . . .

. . . with John and Karin starting year one!

ADVANCED SECTION SUMMARY

1.   Don't begin this section before you're ready . . .

2.   Prepare to find your mate!

3.   From your last 20 dates, write your TOP 3'S.

4.   Compare these TOP 3'S to your old ads.

5.   Create an improved ad using your TOP 3'S.

6.   Insert some of your "I really liked . . . " and "I wish . . . "

7.   Don't worry about the number of replies—now it's quality over quantity!

8.   Always put those who you know won't work in the NO MORE file, regardless of their other great qualities.

9.   Choose your EXCEPTIONAL 3 to focus on.

10.   Date!

11.   After each date, write a DATE RECAP.

12.   If you haven't met your mate, try again, starting at various points according to what you learned from your EXCEPTIONAL 3.

13.   Use common sense.   You're not perfect and neither will be your mate!   CONTINUE if the positives greatly outweigh the negatives!

Most importantly . . .

ENJOY YOURSELF!

THE END FOR US . . .
THE BEGINNING FOR YOU!

11.28.03

01.01.01

At the risk of repeating ourselves:

"The successful are willing to do what the unsuccessful are unwilling to do!"

We hope reading our book helped you become successful!

ABOUT THE AUTHORS:

KARIN STERLING ANDERSON

An in-demand Script Coordinator in the film business, Karin's first job was working with **Elaine May** on her rewrite for **Jerry Bruckheimer's** *Dangerous Minds*, and she continues to work on Bruckheimer films.

She started with director **Tony Scott** on *Crimson Tide* when he hired **Quentin Tarantino** for a rewrite and continues to work with Tony today.

She has written humorous articles about her life and work in Los Angeles that have been published in **"Emmy," "Shape," "Sail"** and **"Los Angeles"** magazines.

In 1999, Karin took a year off to learn how to sail in celebration of her 40th birthday in 2000. She was featured in **"Working Woman," "Sports for Women"** and **"Sail"** magazines.

On TV, she appeared in an **"Amazing Women"** profile for a nationally aired series and also an ABC affiliate profile **"Living Your Dream."**

She lived and worked on her sailboat with her dog Gator until she met her husband, John, using the screen name **"TrueBlueFemme."**

ABOUT THE AUTHORS:

BETH ROBERTS

As Executive Vice President of Business Affairs for **NBC Universal Television**, Beth negotiates deals with all of the major production studios for shows including "**West Wing**," "**Medium**," "**ER**," "**Monk**," "**Battlestar Galactica**," "**Scrubs**," "**Fear Factor**," "**The Apprentice**," "**The Tonight Show with Jay Leno**," and "**Late Night with Conan O'Brien**," to name a few.

Beth speaks around town on entertainment issues in addition to her annual course at **UCLA Extension**, "Business Affairs for Television." She also contributes to an entertainment course at **USC Annenberg School for Communication**.

As a young lawyer, Beth practiced commercial real estate law in New York City, at a 250-attorney law firm. Inspired by Beryl Markham's "West with the Night," she made a radical decision: She quit her job to travel the world.

Beth spent a full year backpacking solo in New Zealand, Australia, Indonesia, Hong Kong, Macau, Thailand, Singapore, India, England, Wales and Scotland. Battling leeches, tigers and would-be lotharios made a career change seem like child's play. On her return, Beth moved to Los Angeles to join the entertainment industry.

Ten years later, she was running business affairs at NBC, but found meeting her mate a challenge. After studying several on-line dating sites and ads, Beth jumped in and posted an ad. She met with 5 men; the 5th is now her husband, Warren.

THE "JUST SHOW ME WHAT TO DO" LOOK

TwyggMedia

Beth and Karin had a vision in their minds but not at their fingertips, so they hired graphic designer Tiffany Sims to create the logo and face of the **"Just Show Me"** girl that you've grown to love. Check out all her cool stuff at www. twyggmedia.com.

CANISAPIEN SOLUTIONS

Beth and Karin wanted to make the online experience as easy and fun as their **Just Show Me What To Do** books. They asked website designer Patricia Nelson to illustrate their vision of a world by and for women where help, hope and feeling good are a few simple clicks away at www. justshowmewhat2do.com. See her brilliance at www. canisapien.com.

For the hundreds of images Beth and Karin needed to make this book simple and fun, they used some clip art licensed from Clip Art, Inc.

Write Correct

Staring at the same words on a page can make you cross-eyed, so Beth and Karin hired proofreader/layout guy David Mandel to help them look good! He can help you,~~to~~ too. Email him at WriteCorrect@gmail.com.

219